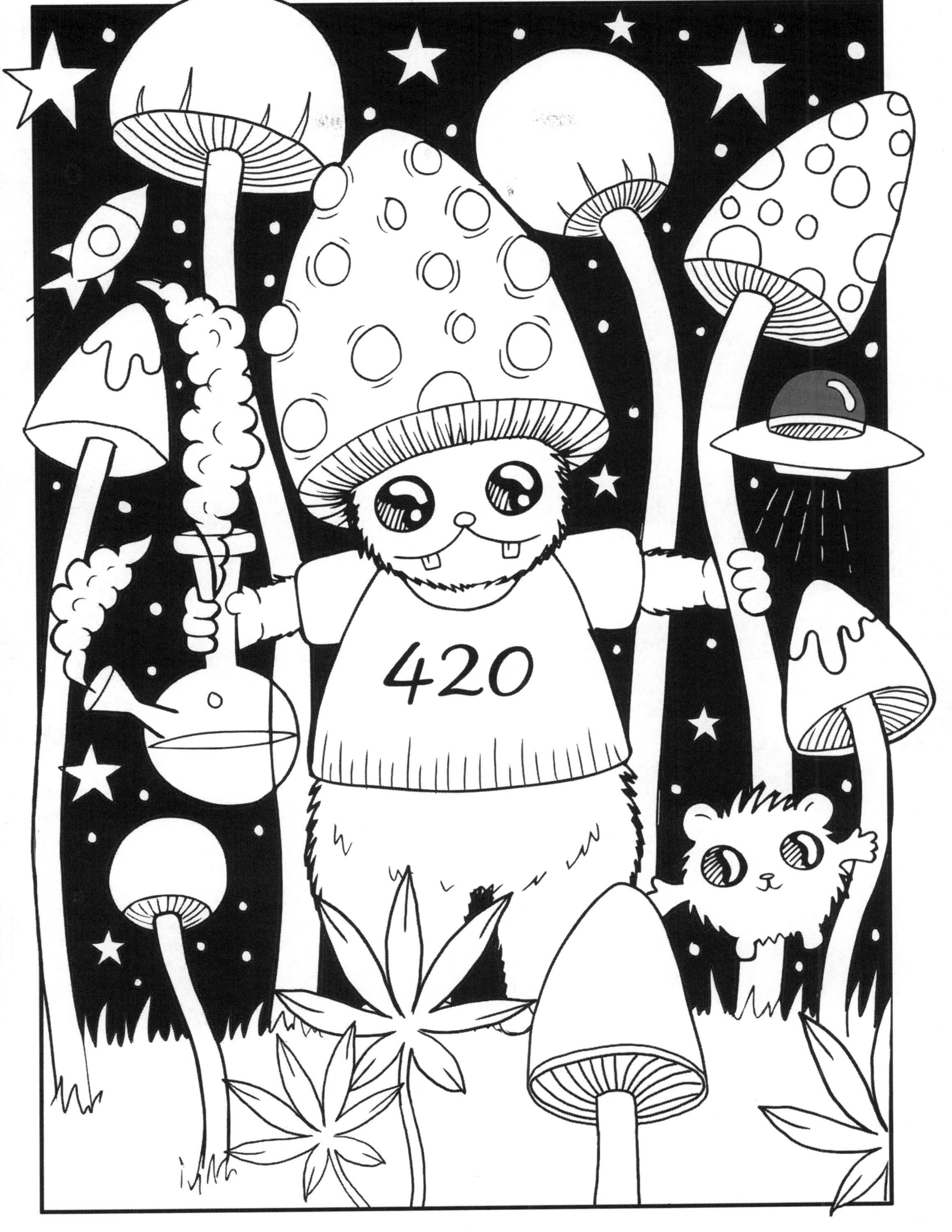
420

Thank you for purchasing STONER COLORING BOOK

by Edwina Mc Namee

You can download the book using the link below:

https://www.edwinamcnamee.com/stoners-pdf

We made the book available using Google Drive. Google Drive allows us to provide high-resolution coloring pages in one PDF file.

All of our books are protected under international copyright law and licensed for your personal use only. You may not share or resell this book. You are welcome to share colored-in pages on social media.

If you are doing a video reveiw of this book please be sure to cover the link
IT IS A COPYRIGHT VIOLATION to share this link

Please let us know if you have any questions:

EDWINAMCNAMEE.COM

Thank you,

Edwina Mc Namee